For D. A. Willis — J.W.

For Nelly — T.R.

Text copyright © Jeanne Willis, 2005. Illustration copyright © Tony Ross, 2005.

This paperback edition first published in 2007 by Andersen Press Ltd.

The rights of Jeanne Willis and Tony Ross to be identified as the author and illustrator of this work have been asserted by them in accordance with the Copyright, Designs and Patents Act, 1988.

First published in Great Britain in 2005 by Andersen Press Ltd., 20 Vauxhall Bridge Road, London SW1V 2SA.

Published in Australia by Random House Australia Pty., 20 Alfred Street, Milsons Point, Sydney, NSW 2061.

All rights reserved.

Colour separated in Switzerland by Photolitho AG, Zürich.

Printed and bound in Italy by Grafiche AZ, Verona.

10   9   8   7   6   5   4   3   2   1

British Library Cataloguing in Publication Data available.

ISBN-13: 978 1 84270 554 4

This book has been printed on acid-free paper

This Book Belong

. . . .

Killer Gorilla

Jeanne Willis   Tony Ross

Andersen Press

There was a mouse who had lost her baby.

She went up the mountain.

Down the mountain.

Round and round the rainforest.
But she still couldn't find him.
The rainforest was very, very big,
And the baby was very, very small.
The mouse thought she'd lost him for ever.

Just when things
couldn't get any worse . . .

Out jumped a great, big, hairy, scary ape!
'It's a Killer Gorilla!' she squeaked.
'Help! Help! He'll catch me!
He'll squash me and scratch me
He'll mince me and mash me
And crunch me up for lunch!'

'Stop!'

bellowed the gorilla.

But the mouse ran and ran.
Over the bridge, over the sea
All the way to China.
But the gorilla was never far behind.
'Who are you running from, Mouse?' asked Panda.
'A Killer Gorilla!' she squeaked,
'Help! Help! He'll catch me!
He'll squash me and scratch me!
He'll mince me and mash me
And crunch me up for lunch!'

'**Stop!**' bellowed the gorilla,
But the mouse ran and ran.
All the way to America.

But the gorilla was catching up.

'Who are you running from, Mouse?' asked Chipmunk.
'A Killer Gorilla,' she squeaked.
'Help! Help! He'll catch me!
He'll squash me and scratch me
He'll mince me and mash me
And crunch me up for lunch!'

'Stop!' bellowed the gorilla.

But the mouse ran and ran.

Into a submarine. Under the sea.
All the way to Australia.

The gorilla had almost caught up.

'Who are you running from,
Mouse?' asked Koala.

'A Killer Gorilla!' she squeaked.
'Help! Help! He'll catch me!
He'll squash me and scratch me
He'll mince me and mash me
And crunch me up for lunch!'

'**Stop!**' bellowed the gorilla.
But the mouse ran and ran,
Across the desert. Into the submarine.
Under the sea. Across the ice.
All the way to the Arctic.
She looked around.

She was all alone . . .

Except for the gorilla!

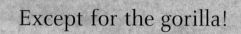

'Stop!'

he bellowed.

The mouse tried to run, but she was too tired.
The snow was so thick and she'd run such a long way.
The gorilla came closer . . .

and closer . . .

And *closer!*

The mouse stood still. She shivered and shut her eyes.
She wished she could see her baby once more
before she was eaten.

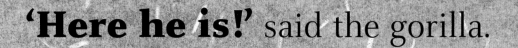
'Here he is!' said the gorilla.

Cradled in his huge hands was the baby mouse.

'I found him in the forest,' said the gorilla.
'I was trying to give him back, but you wouldn't stop!
Who were you running from, Mouse?'

The mouse looked into his kind, brown eyes
and blushed.
'Oh . . . nobody you know!' she squeaked.
'I'm not frightened now.'

'Even so, it's a big, scary world
out there,' said the gorilla.
'Let me carry you home.
You'll feel much safer.'

And the mouse did.

Other titles written by Jeanne Willis
and illustrated by Tony Ross:

Daft Bat

Don't Let Go!

Dozy Mare

I Hate School

I Want To Be A Cowgirl

Manky Monkey

Mayfly Day

Misery Moo

The Really Rude Rhino

Shhh!

Tadpole's Promise

What Did I Look Like When I Was A Baby?

Dr Xargle's Book of Earthlets